Happy Hanukkah!

Written by Cala Spinner
Illustrated by Jason Fruchter

This book is based on the TV series Peppa Pig. Peppa Pig is created by Neville Astley and Mark Baker.
Peppa Pig © Astley Baker Davies Ltd/Entertainment One UK Ltd 2003.

ISBN 978-1-338-61171-7

10 9 8 7 6 5 4 3 2 1
Printed in the U.S.A.

20 21 22 23 24
40

First printing 2020

www.peppapig.com

SCHOLASTIC INC.

Peppa and George are visiting their grandparents.
Peppa smells something wonderful and potato-y.
"I'm making latkes," says Granny Pig. "A latke is a
potato pancake. It's what people eat on Hanukkah."

"What's Hanukkah?" Peppa asks.

"Hanukkah is the Festival of Lights," replies Grandpa Pig. "People celebrate the Festival of Lights all over the world. Tonight, we will celebrate, too."

"Long ago, there wasn't any electricity," says
Granny Pig. "Do you know what uses electricity?"
Peppa thinks about it.
"Television!" she says.

"That's right, Peppa! There wasn't any television. There weren't any light switches, either. Back then, you needed fire to see in the dark."

That gives Peppa an idea.
"Let's play a game," she tells George. "We'll pretend we live long ago, when there was no electricity!"
Peppa turns the light switch off.

It's dark!
"What can we do without light?" Granny Pig asks.

Peppa thinks about it.
Then she gets an idea.
"We can make a fort!"

Together, Peppa and George find cushions, pillows, and a blanket. They build a fort with all of their materials.

But just as Peppa is about to add the finishing touch,
George knocks it down!
"George!" Peppa says. "That wasn't very nice."
Snort, snort! George giggles.

The pillows are everywhere. Peppa can't see them because the lights are off!
"I can't put the fort back together now," Peppa says.

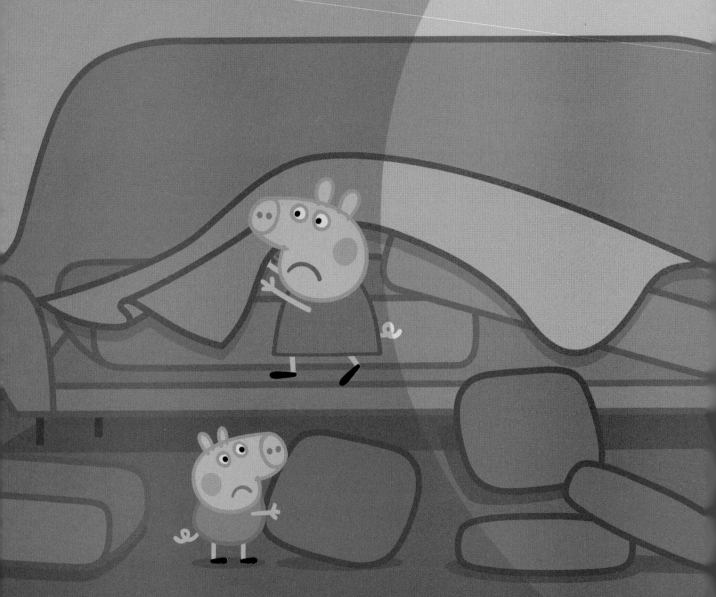

Grandpa Pig has an idea.
"Why don't we light a candle?" he asks.
Grandpa Pig lights a candle, and Peppa and George can see!

Peppa and George start to put the fort back together, but before they're done, the candle has burned through.

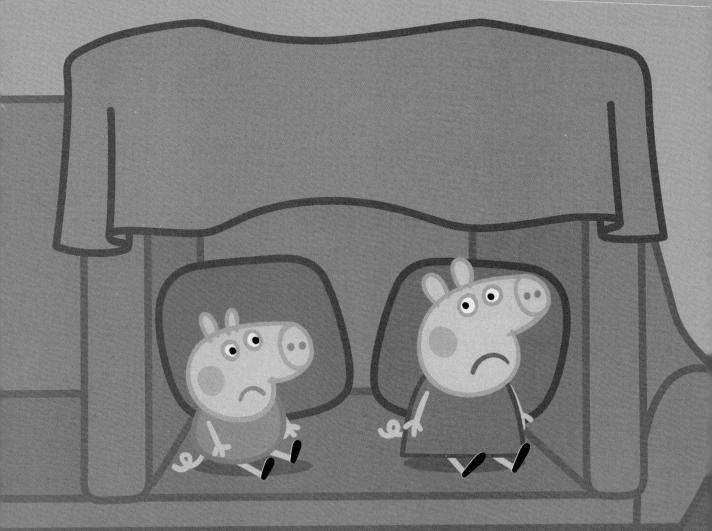

"It must have been very hard to live without electricity," Peppa says.

Granny Pig turns the lights back on.
"Long ago, there was a light that lasted for *eight days*," she says. "We celebrate this miracle by lighting the candles on a menorah. It has eight candles, and each night, a new one is lit."

"Tonight is the eighth night of Hanukkah, so that means . . ." Grandpa Pig starts to say.
"All the candles will be lit!" chimes Peppa.
They also light the tallest candle in the middle. It is called the helper.

"Do you play any games on Hanukkah?" Peppa asks.

"Yes!" Granny Pig says. "One of the games is called *dreidel*. A dreidel is a spinning top. If you win, you get chocolates!"

Peppa and George cheer. They like games! They like chocolates!

Granny Pig gives every player a handful of chocolate coins. They each put one in the middle. Then she spins the dreidel. It lands on a little letter that is called a *nun*.
"A *nun* means I don't get any chocolates," Granny Pig explains. "Now it's the next player's turn."

Grandpa Pig spins the dreidel. He gets a letter called a *shin*.

"Oh no," Grandpa Pig grumbles. "A *shin* means I have to put a chocolate in."

Now it is George's turn. He spins the top.
He gets a letter called a *hay*!
"Well done, George," says Granny Pig. "You
get *half* of the chocolates in the middle!"

Last, it is time for Peppa. She spins the dreidel.
It spins and it spins and it spins . . . and it falls off the table!
"Oh no," Peppa says. "Does that mean I don't get any chocolates?"

"Go look, Peppa," says Granny Pig. "What did the dreidel land on?"

Peppa crawls under the table. It's a *gimel*!

"That means you win all the chocolates in the middle!" Grandpa Pig says.

Peppa smiles. "I love Hanukkah!" she says.

Happy Hanukkah!

Hanukkah

Hanukkah is the Festival of Lights. It is celebrated in the Hebrew month of *Kislev*, which usually falls in November or December.

People celebrate Hanukkah in lots of different ways. They always celebrate the miracle of light.

On Hanukkah, a special candle holder called a *menorah* is used. On the first night, only one candle is lit. On the second night, only two. By the eighth night, all candles are lit.

The candle in the middle of the menorah is called the *shamash*. That means "helper" in Hebrew. People use this candle to light the other ones, from right to left.

Many families eat latkes, jelly doughnuts, and other food that's covered in oil to remember the oil that burned for eight days.

Families also play *dreidel*, or spinning top. This can be played with candy, cookies, or even gold coins!

Some families also give gifts on each night of Hanukkah. Often, those gifts include money or donations for those who need it.